P9-BZS-069

DISCARD

E
Joo   Joosse,Barbara
         Better With Two

3633

Irving School Learning Center

BETTER WITH TWO

by Barbara M. Joosse

illustrations by Catherine Stock

HARPER & ROW, PUBLISHERS

3633
Irving School Learning Center

Better With Two

Text copyright © 1988 by Barbara M. Joosse
Illustrations copyright © 1988 by Catherine Stock
Printed in Singapore. All rights reserved.
Typography by Bettina Rossner.
10   9   8   7   6   5   4   3   2   1
First Edition

Library of Congress Cataloging-in-Publication Data
Joosse, Barbara M.
   Better with two/by Barbara M. Joosse: illustrated by
Catherine Stock.—1st ed.
        p.   cm.
   Summary: Laura tries to make Mrs. Brady feel better when
her dog Max dies.
   ISBN 0-06-023076-2 : $
   ISBN 0-06-023077-0 (lib. bdg.): $
   [1. Friendship—Fiction.   2. Death—Fiction.]   I. Stock.
Catherine, ill.   II. Title.
PZ7.J7435Be 1988   87-30652
[E]—dc19   CIP
                                                          AC

Finally for Pete, who made my life
Better With Two
B. M. J.

For Charlene and Augie
C. S.

Mrs. Brady and Max live in the yellow house next to Laura's. Every morning, while Laura rides her bike, Mrs. Brady and Max take a walk. They walk slowly, because Max is very old.

"We walk at ten o'clock, punctually," Mrs. Brady says.

Mrs. Brady wears a hat with a feather on it. When it's windy, she keeps one hand on her hat. Max wears a red plaid coat with M A X on the side in green sequined letters.

After their walk, Mrs. Brady and Max
have tea. Mrs. Brady calls tea
elevenses because she lived in
England when she was young. And in
England, morning tea is called
elevenses.

On special days, Laura joins them.

Mrs. Brady and Laura have tea with
milk, and cookies or fancy little cakes.

Max has tea out of his own china cup
with a wide top so he can reach in
to drink. He eats his dog biscuit from
a paper doily.

"Max has perfect manners," Mrs. Brady
says. "He never spills a drop of tea nor
leaves a crumb of biscuit."

Max likes it when Laura scratches the
fuzzy spot behind his ears.
It's always itchy.

After elevenses, Laura goes home.
Then Mrs. Brady and Max sit
on the porch swing and watch
the neighborhood.

They sit next to each other and rock
back and forth, back and forth. Mrs.
Brady pushes the swing with her foot,
sometimes in time to the music from
her radio.

Often, they sing.

Max likes "I've Been Working on the
Railroad" best.

Sometimes Max jumps carefully off the swing to growl at a squirrel or bark at the mailman.

Sometimes Mrs. Brady does needlework.

One day Mrs. Brady sits on the porch
swing without Max. She and Max don't
take a walk that day, and they don't
have elevenses.

"Where's Max?" Laura asks Mama.

"Max died," Mama says.

Laura thinks of Max in his red plaid coat. She thinks of the fuzzy spot behind his ear, and not scratching it anymore.

When Laura cries, Mama hugs her till she's finished. "Crying is better with two," Mama says.

Irving School Learning Center

After lunch, Mrs. Brady is still on the porch swing. She sits in different places, but no matter where she sits the swing rocks crooked. It doesn't work very well with one.

Mrs. Brady looks lonely and very sad.

Laura brings Mrs. Brady a little china dog that looks just like Max.

"Thank you," says Mrs. Brady as Laura walks home.

The next day Laura brings Mrs. Brady
some flowers—clover and dandelions
and fluffy grass that looks like feathers.

"Thank you," says Mrs. Brady as Laura
walks home.

The next day Laura brings Mrs. Brady
a drawing. It's full of happy things—
a rainbow and a smiling sun, a paper
doily and a teacup.

"Thank you," says Mrs. Brady as Laura
walks home.

Laura watches Mrs. Brady on her porch swing. She rocks back and forth, crooked. The flowers, the drawing and the little china dog are all on the porch. And still, Mrs. Brady looks sad.

Laura thinks. She thinks of Mrs. Brady missing Max. She thinks of walks and elevenses and swinging alone when you are lonely.

Finally, Laura remembers crying with Mama, and she thinks of one more thing she can do.

Laura packs a brown paper bag, and
runs next door to sit with Mrs. Brady
on the porch swing. They rock back and
forth, together. Back and forth, back
and forth for a very long time.

Now the porch swing rocks straight,
because swinging, like crying, is better
with two.

Now Mrs. Brady doesn't look so sad.

When she checks her watch, Mrs. Brady
sits up straight and says, "Why, Laura!
We've almost forgotten tea."

"I haven't forgotten," says Laura.
She opens her brown paper bag
and pulls out two windmill cookies.
One for herself, and one for her friend.

Then, because it is a very special day,
Laura and Mrs. Brady go inside for
elevenses.